Chapter One

IT WAS APRIL holiday time when the Jones family moved to London from their Cornish home. Dad's small local business had failed, and the only work he could find was up in town.

"Beastly, grimy place," moaned Jen.

"Worse still, no animals," muttered Jamie.

"No freedom. No riding Pepper on the moor."

"Nothing but smelly cars. No throwing sticks for Barrel."

"Nothing to do."

"Nothing."

I

"Oh, twins, please stop whingeing!" Mum was in despair. "Can't you find anything to do? Try out that adventure playground?"

Jen snorted.

"So boring, without my dog," grumbled Jamie.

Barrel was his friend, his fat shaggy mongrel, found wandering on the moor three years ago. Dad had promptly called him "that barrel of fur", so Barrel he became.

"Best dog you could ever meet," Jamie told everyone. "Look at that smile, look at that super tail. What sort of dog is he, Dad?"

"A surprise. I reckon a Dandy Dinmont met a Wolfhound."

Barrel was an odd shape, with a big head, large plump long-haired body on very short legs, and a grand flourish of wolfish tail. He was clumsy and took up plenty of room.

"Much too much for a ground-floor flat with a tiny patch of garden that's mostly mud and bramble," said Dad.

So Barrel had been given to Mr Bates the butcher; and Jamie still wept each night for Barrel's soft coat and wet black nose and the whole warm friendly fuggy smell of him.

"Adventure playgrounds! After my Pepper?" moaned Jen. Pepper was a small stout moorland pony with a peppery temper. It was no comfort to Jen that her friend Pamela would be riding Pepper, jogging up and down the Cornish lanes.

"Parents are the pits," she told Jamie fiercely. "Why couldn't Dad have found a job near home?"

Mum had overheard. "Hey, that's enough! You don't know how lucky we are, you ungrateful pair, or how hard it is to find work these days. Go on out and get some air."

They went reluctantly but soon

drifted back indoors, squabbling.

"The twins never used to fight," Mum said sadly. "And they're looking dreadful – Jen stuffs herself with chips and ices, Jamie eats next to nothing."

"What's the matter with them?" Dad asked snappily. He felt tired and overworked.

"I'm afraid they're missing Barrel and Pepper."

"How can we help it? Local kids keep hamsters or goldfish. Pepper and Barrel, here! It's crazy. They might keep a cat – though even cats cost money."

Jen came in, sucking toffee. Her cheeks bulged, covered with spots. Jamie had a cold. He sneezed and sneezed.

"Colds in spring, I ask you," Dad groaned.

"Dad says, would you like a cat?" said Mum hopefully.

"A dear little fluffy fluffy kitten, like that dear little fluffy girl next door?" muttered Jen. Mrs Jones looked at her and replied crisply, "Don't be silly." She was quite glad when the twins went into the living room and slammed the door.

Jamie flung open the window and leaned out. The garden looked so empty without a dog in it . . .

At least there was an animal of sorts: on the wall.

"Look, Jen – just look at that amazing cat!"

It was a bruiser of a tom, furred in ginger and marigold stripes, tail long and thick as an Italian sausage. His eyes, greengage-colour with ebony slit pupils, watched them with an

unblinking stare. He would have been
a noble cat, if he hadn't been too thin
and scarred from many battles.

"Bet he's hungry, Jen. Come on,
let's go talk to him."

They ran outside. The cat watched
them coming, flicking the tip of an
arrogant tail, flattening his ears,
arching his back. He spat.

"Don't be so mean. Can't you see we're friends?" Jamie pushed through the brambles. He stretched up a hand to stroke the cat. Quick as a flash a yellow paw struck out, tipped with what felt like sharpened thorns.

"*Wow!*" Several raspberry-red stripes marked the back of Jamie's hand, oozing crimson beads. He licked them away. "He's wild, not like most idiot cats. I like him – shall we tame him?"

"He's got a nasty temper – and he's someone else's."

"Bet he's a stray, he's so thin. Bet someone turned him out."

"They had reason to, with those claws! I'm going in."

"Bring something out for him to eat," Jamie called after her. "Mum's been shopping."

"Oh, all right." Jen made a face. She went into the kitchen to rummage halfheartedly in the fridge, and found some liver intended for tomorrow's lunch. She snipped a bit off it, keeping one eye on Mum.

"What are you looking for, Jen? No more ices today."

"Just looking . . . " Jen slid hurriedly from the room.

The cat tossed the liver about as though it was a mouse, then gobbled it greedily. A deep rumbling purr almost shook the wall, but he moved aside when Jamie tried to stroke him again. The paw threatened.

"He's splendid," said Jamie. "Tough. I'm going to keep him."

"Hah! You'll see." Jen went back into the house. What was a battle-scarred cat, however fine, compared with Pepper?

"Come and help me with supper, love. I'll never finish this lot in time." Mum's face was flushed, her hair on end. She'd organized her time badly today. Once the twins were at school things should be easier, there would be time for her computer graphics course.

Jamie disappeared from the house till dinner time. He came back late from the corner store, which sold everything from spices and wine to chilled food and hardware. He was clutching a parcel, and put it down beside his plate.

"Something special for my cat," he explained.

"Your cat, Jamie? Already?" said Dad.

"It's a yellow thing that spits," said Jen. "Grotty."

"He's not. He was sitting on our wall, Dad." Jamie put the parcel beneath his chair. It was strange – Jen used to share his likes and dislikes. Here in London she seemed different.

After supper, he retrieved the parcel and went outside. There was no sign of the cat, but Jamie was hopeful – this was obviously part of its own territory, there was no mistaking that strong musky tomcat smell. He unwrapped his parcel and took out a small scarlet collar and a tight bundle of plastic straw, the kind that gets wrapped round new china.

Half-hidden among brambles was a rotting rabbit hutch. Jamie opened its door and wiped the floor carefully with a bunch of weeds. He scattered the straw about before returning to the house for a saucer of milk and scraps of meat.

Everything ready, he sat down to wait.

He waited a long while, shivering in the cold and damp of dusk. Through the living room window he could see the greenish flicker of the television. He began to wonder what Jen was watching. Pity she didn't like the cat. . .

Then the tomcat came, mincing on tiger paws along the wall. He sniffed, whiskers bristling, aware of something unusual about his territory. He found the milk and crouched beside it, shoulders hunched, tail twitching. He began to lap hungrily.

"Cat! Here, cat – " Jamie stood up and walked forward cautiously, holding out a scrap of meat. His other hand held the collar ready. But in two seconds the cat was gone, springing along the wall on nimble pads and sending the milk saucer flying.

"Oh, *no*," breathed Jamie. He waited a while longer but the cat didn't return. And the saucer was broken. Worse still, it was one of Mum's best. He crept back into the

house and hid the broken pieces
beneath a pile of kitchen china.

In the living room Dad was working
at a table while Mum and Jen were
watching television: dancers lumping
about in some idiot ballet. Boring.

"Jen – " Jamie made their old secret
sign of two crossed fingers which
meant "want to tell you something",
but she shook her head and went on
watching the screen. It was baffling.

Dad said, "In or out, Jamie?
Whichever it is, shut the door."

He went and sat on his bed.

"It's only a fool cat. If it had been
Barrel, now . . . " He stared bleakly at
the floor. Everything was so empty
without Barrel, and Jen and he were
starting at their new school next week.
He'd be lost without his friend Paul
too, who had always helped him with

his maths. It was bound to be the pits
– a laugh a minute. Huh.

At breakfast next day, Jen was all
smiles, which made matters worse.

"Letter from Pamela!" She waved it
at Jamie, as Mum handed round plates
of cereal. "She's asked me to stay next
holidays and ride Pepper. She says
Pepper's missing me and is really mine
still, and her dad will borrow another
pony for her to ride."

"Her father's lucky, still doing so
well," sighed Dad.

Jamie pushed his plate aside. Lucky
Jen, all right. She didn't mind at all
that he'd have holidays alone in
London, with no Barrel. What sort of a
twin was that?

"You'll need to shed some fat or
Pepper's legs will bend," he sniffed.

"Now, Jamie, that's enough!" said Mum. "He has a point, though, Jen. You've put on too much weight, stuffing yourself with ices."

"I'll eat fruit instead," Jen promised. "Will there be games at school?"

Games? thought Jamie. They'd always hated organized games. She's not my twin any more – she's just one big mistake.

Chapter Two

JEN TOOK TO the new school at once – everything was OK, now Pepper was waiting for her. She was sorry about Barrel, but Jamie's sulkiness couldn't be allowed to spoil everything when there was so much going on at school: gymnastics, and swimming at the Council baths, which was great.

"Nothing seems half so bad here as we thought, does it?" she said to Jamie.

He stared at her coldly. She might be his twin, but she could be very thick sometimes.

"Hurry up, Jen Jones – baseball!" yelled a tall girl with huge legs and plaited hair, and Jen rushed away without a second thought. "Coming too, Jamie?" bawled the girl, like a foghorn. But he shook his head and went to sit by the bushes at the far end of the playground.

There was another boy sitting there all by himself, rolling marbles to and fro in the dust.

"What's your name?" he asked, after a while.

"Jamie."

"Mine's Malik." He rolled a marble at Jamie, who rolled it back and wished he'd go away.

"Have a game?"

"Oh, all right."

They had one, and then another. Malik didn't seem too bad, in fact

Jamie rather liked him. He was thin and dark with large brown eyes and a ready smile.

"Don't you play games?"

"Not that sort. I like chess. I'm clever. That's why they put me up a year at school. Some of the other boys don't like me because of that," said Malik simply.

"I like animals a lot better than people. They don't play idiot games," growled Jamie.

Malik laughed. "You sound like my old grandfather. He likes animals, and that's the sort of thing he says when he's feeling cross. You'd better come and meet him – he lives with us, me and my mother and father. My father owns the corner store."

"I bought some things there last week. Thought I'd seen you somewhere."

"I was behind the counter, reading," said Malik. "I remember you coming in."

"Your dad was pretty good to me. I bought a leather collar, and he gave me some straw; they're for a huge ginger cat. A stray, I think. Wild, and thin."

Malik seemed interested. "Oh, I know him. Some people moved away and dumped him. He lives on the rough patch up beyond the station. He's wily – even the RSPCA can't catch him."

"I like him. I'm going to keep him."

"You'll be so lucky! Why do you want to, anyway?"

Jamie hesitated, then told him about Barrel.

"Must be really bad without him," said Malik, and Jamie liked him even more. "At least you've got a sister, though. She looks OK. Wish I had one."

"She's my twin, and she *used* to be OK. But she's changed. She *likes* this ghastly, boring school."

"I used to bunk off but it got pretty dull, alone," said Malik. "You could bunk off with me if you liked."

Jamie felt rather alarmed. "I dunno . . . we'd need to be careful." He thought it over. "Well – if I did, would you help me catch the cat?"

"If you'll play chess with me."

"I don't know how."

"I'll teach you. My father's too busy to play much, and my grandfather's so old he goes to sleep."

Jamie nodded, cautiously. "I'll think about it," he said.

It wasn't long before Jamie found the idea of bunking off was growing on him.

On the first fine day that came along, Malik and he took their school lunch boxes up the wild Patch beyond the station. It was large, like a small common. There was a huddle of birch trees, even gorse bushes that smelt nutty in the hot sun like Cornish cliffs and made Jamie homesick. There was also a dump of old tyres and tin cans, plastic rubbish, and a broken bench where old men slept.

"It's bad up here at night," Malik told Jamie. "Rough."

Jamie lay on his back and stared up at the sky through joined fingers. From the corner of his eyes he could see peeling houses and crumbly high-rise flats. Far above him, to his surprise, a hawk hovered. Luckily, it was the only thing that seemed to be watching them. He kept expecting someone from the school to appear – or even Dad.

That hawk's wild, like me . . . from the country, he thought. We're not right here, we're in prison.

But the hawk was free, it could go where it liked, really. Fool hawk, to stay. Jamie sighed.

"How do we find my cat?"

"Yours?" Malik laughed. He was always laughing. He didn't seem to mind town life one bit. Or to be nervous about being caught. "We don't find him. We lie low and wait for him."

"That's feeble." Jamie wanted action. He drew the collar from his pocket.

"He'll hate you if you try to put that on him."

"I was going to start taming him at home."

"I should make friends first. That's what grandfather would say."

Malik drew out a carved box from his school bag.

"What's that?"

"My pocket chess set."

"What a con! We don't need crazy games outdoors."

"The cat will come if he sees we're doing something else. He's nosy."

Malik began setting out the game.

"My father says chess teaches you to think. It's really good fun, too. Here's a knight, and this one's called a rook."

"Doesn't look like a bird. More like a castle."

"It *is* a castle – *rukh* means castle in Persian, but it turned into rook. It's a very ancient game, Maharajahs played it in India with sets of gold and silver. This large piece here's the queen. She's more powerful than any other piece. She's like my mother!" Malik grinned.

Jamie sighed again. Malik was showing off, but at least to learn about chess would be one up on Jen.

Later, they shared lunch boxes: chicken tikka and poppadams, egg and lettuce sandwiches, bananas. After a while the cat peered from the bushes and watched them.

Jamie was thrilled. "I brought a fish finger for him – " He laid it at arm's length on the grass.

"That's why your banana tasted foul. Another game?"

Reluctantly, Jamie began setting out his chessmen as Malik had shown him, while the cat emerged from the bushes and started washing himself in the sun, giving special care to his soft pale belly fur. Suddenly he made a forward pounce on to the fish finger, and swallowed it ravenously. Then he took

courage and began trying to get the
top off Malik's lunch box.

"He's still hungry. Clever, too,"
whispered Jamie, as the lid came off.
"Did he ever have a name?"

"Ginger."

Jamie snorted. "Let's think of
something better – he's a grand cat.
Like a – an emperor."

"Napoleon?" suggested Malik.

"Doesn't look French, stupid."

"He's popular with she-cats, though.
My mother's friends got tired of him
wailing outside their houses, and sick
of ginger kittens."

"We'll call him Sultan, then. Sultans
had plenty of wives."

Sultan had finished with the lunch
box and came strolling over to fix
Jamie with a greengage stare.

"Look at that! He knows his name."

"He knows he wants more food, anyway."

"Not today, Sultan." Jamie put out a hand, and the cat fled into the bushes. Jamie was downcast. "He's gone! Bet he won't come back again."

Malik shrugged. "He will another day – if he smells more fish."

"We can't keep bunking off, though."

"Why not? It's a huge class. No one noticed before, till I cut the Head's class: he was more clued in."

"What happened then?"

"Just extra work; kept in. But my father got to hear of it, and beat me."

Jamie eyed him, wondering if his casual tone was genuine.

"Anyway," said Malik, "our teachers are bunking off quite a lot themselves, hadn't you noticed? It's some dispute. *And* we've got this new Head – with luck she won't have heard about me. Anyway, she goes in for *caring*, ha-ha." He grinned wickedly. "Come on, J., we'd better go. If we slide back in for the last class they won't notice we weren't there."

Chapter Three

THEY WERE CAREFUL for a week or two. Then, since they had got away with it, bunking off gradually became a habit. "Another wildcat strike today?" Malik would murmur in Jamie's ear. Missing school didn't affect his place in class, while Jamie's own slid lower and lower till he was only one seat from the door.

Malik had been proved right – shortage of staff was in their favour. Although word went round among the pupils that it was odd to see Jen Jones do so well when her twin brother was so thick.

"I don't care," Jamie told Malik. "And it's pretty thick to wear that pink jumpsuit for trampolining. Yuk!"

If Jen wanted to go off and do things on her own, well, let her – that jumpsuit might have scared Sultan off for good. Now when Jamie went up to the Patch the ginger cat came to greet him purring, but it was a beggar's purr, for food. His refusal to be friends was like a nagging toothache.

"What else do you expect of sultans?" asked Malik. "He thinks you're his cook!"

"Barrel wouldn't be like that."

Jamie longed all the more for Barrel. How could a dog like him be happy with old Mr Bates? He'd get fatter still with all those bones and pickings, and no long walks to keep him in his best Barrel shape . . .

Some days, if it began to rain, Sultan simply gulped the food and crept back into his hiding place.

"This is *worse* than boring," exclaimed Malik, on one such day. "Come on, let's go to the Leisure Centre. Fruit machines are better fun than ginger cats."

"Should we?" Jamie hesitated.

"You're chicken!"

"I'm not," said Jamie indignantly, "but – "

"Just get out quick if I pinch you, see?"

"Why?"

"Bit rough round here, you know."

Jamie didn't, but wouldn't let on to Malik who seemed so streetwise. Maybe he was just showing off again, like he did about chess. People were so difficult. Barrel wouldn't show off, not him. Jamie sighed, and went on poking around in the undergrowth, hoping to flush out Sultan.

"Hurry up." Malik danced in impatience. "It's raining cats and dogs!"

"Hasn't rained my cat, though. *Sul-tan!*"

"Forget him – I'm soaked. Do let's go to the Centre now – I got my pocket money today. *Jamie.*"

"OK." Jamie emerged reluctantly, backwards and gorse-prickled. "We'll have to use your money, though, because mine's run out."

Rain had ceased by the time they reached the Centre, though the arcade with the fruit machines was still crowded with people who'd been sheltering from the weather.

Malik and Jamie found a good game in a quiet corner and played it on and on without success until the pocket money was almost gone. Then Malik managed to line up six enemy spaceships in a row and shot them down, ping, ping, ping! Inside the machine a tinny space voice growled 'Total surrender'. There was a sudden great rattling noise and a stream of coins shot out.

"We won, we won! I've got the jackpot!" yelled Malik.

"Won it, did you?" sneered a voice behind them. "Machine stuck, more likely."

"That's right, Sid," agreed another voice. "Kid should give it back. Come on, kid, hand over. We'll see the owner gets it safe." A hand shot out to grab Malik by the collar and twist it tight.

34

"Uh-*uh*," Malik choked.

"Let go of him!" Jamie quavered,
putting up his fists. But he was
knocked aside as the arcade manager
loomed up beside them, growling,
"Out, you lot. No fighting in
here."

"They're stealing his cash!" shouted Jamie.

But the manager didn't want to know. He didn't like kids winning jackpots. "Outside, I said. All of you, or I'll ring the police."

"Run!" Jamie seized Malik by the hand.

They ran puffing and panting from the arcade, down the High Street and up a turning with the gang in pursuit. Out of sight of gaping passers-by they were pounced on and Malik's pockets emptied. With a final kick the bullies left him face downward in the muddy gutter, sobbing. Jamie, who had fought wildly in defence, felt bruised all over.

"You all right?" he gasped.

"I hurt my head," sobbed Malik. "On the kerb."

Jamie helped him up. The cut on

Malik's forehead was pulsing blood
and he was shivering. Jamie put an
arm round him, not knowing what to
do. Did Malik need a hospital? He
didn't know where to find one.
Anyway, the thought of going there
without Mum or Dad was appalling.

"I want to go home, I want to go
home," sobbed Malik. His face was
streaming blood and tears.

"All right, I'll take you there. Here, keep my hankie pressed hard over your cut."

It was some job steering Malik home. Blood got in his eyes so that his walk wobbled from side to side. Now and then people stopped to ask if they could help, but Jamie turned down the offer of a car ride home. (Mum said don't ever take lifts from strangers: not *ever*.)

"He fell down . . . no thanks . . . he's going home," Jamie repeated again and again. When they reached the shop he could have cried too, from relief.

There were three customers waiting inside. They stared as Malik stumbled in, supported by Jamie's arm and wailing something in another language. A stout woman in a floaty sort of dress shot out from behind the counter. From the way she began hugging Malik and carrying on, Jamie guessed she must be his mum, the Chess Queen. She was wailing as loudly as he was. Two of the customers joined in out of sympathy, and the third quietly helped himself to a jar of jam.

Now would be a good time to shove off, thought Jamie, before someone started asking why they weren't at school; but just then Malik's father came into the shop, to discover Malik bleeding and Jamie with one eye closed. He began shaking Jamie to and fro, shouting, "A great boy like you to strike our little Malik!"

"I didn't – ow! Gang – bullies – wah! I brought him – *help!* – back."

It was a while before they got things sorted out, after Malik had managed some explanation in his other language. Then the Chess Queen seized hold of Jamie to hug and kiss him too, before Malik was borne off to be washed and plastered in the bathroom.

"Very, very sorry for unfortunate mistake," said Malik's father, pressing bags of sweets into Jamie's hand, and bars of chocolate into his pocket. "Come, I close the shop early today, and we will see about your eye."

"They're a great lot, your family," Jamie told Malik, an hour later.

It was so comfortable in their back room. Malik's aged grandfather, in a turban and fierce beard, was sitting there, chatting with a younger friend. Jamie had been given two kinds of ice-cream, and the Chess Queen herself had put something wonderfully soothing on his eye, and told him he was a hero, and always welcome in their home.

Soon Jamie found himself telling Malik's grandfather all about Barrel and how much he missed him, almost as though he'd known the old man all his life.

"Very, very terrible, to lose so great a friend," said Grandfather. "I, too, lost my good friend, Akbar – two years ago, now." He shook his head sadly, and they sighed together.

"What sort of a dog was Akbar?"

"An Afghan hound – you know them? Very wonderful dogs. Long legs, long silky hair, a tail like a maharajah's plume."

"No one ever had a better tail than Barrel," said Jamie firmly.

"Since you love animals so, Jamie, you should visit my friend here, Mr Pradesh, in his surgery," suggested grandfather. "He is a vet, and looks after the pets of all the people around here."

"Certainly he must come one day to watch me treat my patients," agreed

Mr Pradesh. "You would like that, Jamie? Yes?"

"Oh, yes. And could you show me how to tame a wild cat?"

Mr Pradesh laughed. "You know of wildcats round here?"

"He's not a real wildcat – just a cat gone wild. I've fed him and talked to him but he won't be friends."

"Well, now," Mr Pradesh looked serious. "Perhaps he just wants to live wild; cats are very independent creatures – we have to let them live as they wish, you know."

"Nobody let me," said Jamie sadly.

Malik's father looked at the clock and got up from his chair.

"Shop can remain closed now, Jamie," he said. "I will walk home with you, to tell your mother and father how good you are to Malik.

How bravely you fought off those boys at school."

"I shouldn't do that!" said Jamie, alarmed. (What had Malik said?)

"It is the least he can do, when we think how you save our little Malik." The Chess Queen hugged him again. "Very fortunate it is not so bad, this cut, now the bleeding stops. That great boy to knock Malik down in playground was too bad."

"You pathetic idiot," hissed Jamie in Malik's ear. "Why tell them that?"

"Don't want to be beaten, so don't you split on us," hissed back Malik. "I gave you a great write-up, anyway."

"You will take his parents that big fruit-and-nut cake with the cherries," the Chess Queen instructed her husband. "Some chilled pies, and oranges too."

"Wine, perhaps? Two bottles?"

"One," said the Chess Queen firmly.

Jamie was glad there was going to be some limit, or he could certainly see questions being asked.

Malik and his mum, Grandfather and Mr Pradesh, all stood outside the store to wave Jamie and Malik's father goodbye. "Do not forget surgery," Mr Pradesh called after them. "It is six o'clock on Monday, Wednesday and Friday evenings, and nine o'clock on Saturday mornings."

"I'll come all right. Thanks!" said Jamie. He might need surgery himself if Dad found out what had really happened.

"I don't believe one word of it," said Jen after supper. "It smells fishy."

"Now Jen, that's enough," Mum chided her. "Dad and I are very pleased Jamie acted so well."

"Perhaps you'd have time for a few words with their Headteacher tomorrow about this bullying?" Dad asked Mum. "I told Malik's father that we would – he's too busy to go himself tomorrow, and his wife sometimes lets her tongue run away with itself, he says."

Jamie shuddered. Mum talk to the Head about something that never happened? That would be checkmate to everyone, all right.

"Please not!" he gasped. "The other kids would call me a supergrass!"

"I must, Jamie, but don't worry about it," said Mum. "I'll be very tactful."

Jen gazed at him with a piercing eye. "Come on, J., let's go down the garden, see if your ginger friend's out there."

"OK, come clean," she told him, when they were standing by the wall. "*I* saw no fighting in the playground – didn't see you there, either. In fact, you've been missing quite often. Don't think I didn't notice."

"Promise you won't split on me?" pleaded Jamie.

"Idiot. Of course I won't. Go on, tell."

Jen's eyes grew larger as she listened to his story. "You are a pair, I must say. Wish you'd told me, I'd have come too. I rather fancy Malik."

"But you'd changed, Jen," Jamie explained. "And you didn't seem to care about Barrel, once it was all right for you with Pepper."

"Sorry – I *was* mean about it. I'll

48

write to Pamela tomorrow and ask her to find out how Barrel is."

"Jen, would you?" Jamie felt better. This was more how his twin should be.

"You'll be in a dreadful mess tomorrow, if Mum comes up to school," Jen reminded him gravely.

Jamie groaned. "I know . . . and Malik, too. He said all those fool things because his dad beats him sometimes. Then it was too late." He groaned again. "Do think of something to put Mum off."

They both thought hard, without success.

"Well, cheer up, it may not be as bad as you think," said Jen, as they walked back together to the house. "Shall I come and meet Malik's family with you one day? It sounds quite good fun at their house."

Chapter Four

THAT NIGHT JAMIE found it hard to sleep – and when he did, he dreamt that Malik's father was chasing him and Barrel across the Patch, pelting them with oranges. Wham! – he got a bullseye on Barrel with the fruit cake, just as Jamie woke to hear Mum calling, "Breakfast, *Jamie*! You'll be late!"

Malik didn't come to school at all that morning. Jamie was glad that Mum didn't fuss like the Chess Queen; and she was always so busy, perhaps she'd forget all about Dad's suggestion.

Could he be so lucky? But at ten o'clock he looked through the classroom window and saw her coming through the gates. It seemed hours before she left again.

When it was time for morning break one of the monitors approached him, saying, "Jamie Jones, you're to go and see the Head straight away."

The bottom of his stomach felt as though it had dropped like a lift, leaving him behind. Scuffing his feet, he went slowly upstairs to the Headteacher's office.

"Sit down, Jamie," she said. "We must have a little talk, mustn't we?" She gave a smile which was probably meant to be reassuring, and waited.

"Oh . . . *argh*!" went Jamie like a bullfrog. He sneezed. He could always sneeze when he wanted to. The Head went on waiting, so he went on sneezing. Then he blew his nose and wiped his face, and stared at his new shoes.

"Jamie!" Her voice had sharpened. He jerked upright.

"Your mother has been up to see me. She was quite right to come. Of course we must put a stop to bullying in school. Who were these boys who set on you and Malik?"

"'Fraid I – I dunno the names."

"Well, you could point them out to me, at least?" She rose, placed a hand on his shoulder, and walked him over to the window which overlooked the playground.

"Well, Jamie?"

"I can't – can't see them! Haven't been here long . . . don't know them all."

"But they don't all look alike to you,
do they?"

"Well, yes. They do, a bit." He
wriggled.

"Come now, you mustn't be
afraid."

"I'm not! It's not that, at all."

"Mmm – " The Head released him. She went back to her desk and looked him over. "That was quite a nasty eye, wasn't it? And you never saw who gave it to you?"

Jamie blushed, and stood on one leg.

"Didn't Malik cry out when he was pushed over and hurt himself?"

At last – something he *could* answer. "Oh yes. Yelled like anything, Malik did."

"It's funny I heard nothing – my window was wide open yesterday."

"There's often noise out there," explained Jamie hurriedly. "And – and we were outside the gates. After school." That was true, at least.

"Why didn't you help him back inside then, and call a teacher?"

Jamie took a deep breath. "He was crying. He cut his head when he fell over. The others ran off and he wanted to go home. So I took him."

The Headteacher looked worried. "If anything like that happens again, you must come straight to us. Promise me, Jamie?"

He nodded.

"I don't really like to encourage my children to tell tales, but you're sure there's nothing else you can say about what happened?"

He shook his head.

"Very well . . . Now our teachers' dispute is over, I'll make sure they keep a careful watchful eye on you and Malik during class. The monitors can too, during break. Perhaps someone could walk home with you." She glanced at the clock. "I'll speak to the whole school about bullying, tomorrow morning. Break's over, you can go back to your lessons now."

He reached the door in a rush.

"And Jamie – "

"Er – yes?" He clutched at the door handle for support.

"I've been looking at your marks. They are not very good, unlike your clever twin's. We must try for improvement, mustn't we?"

She can't really know, thought Jamie. She must just be probing. That's what Malik would call a *caring* look. Hope he doesn't come unstuck if she grills him too.

"Oh yes, I'll try," he promised.

He dived through the doorway before she could ask anything else. She hesitated, then picked up the telephone and rang the corner store, where Malik's father was busy serving customers. Grandfather answered the phone, holding the receiver gingerly to his deaf ear. A soft female voice clucked at him. He strained to hear.

"Malik? . . . Better, better . . . Most kind to ask. Cut very very slight, but much blood. No need to worry . . . goodbye."

He shuffled through into the living room, where Malik was watching television and eating chocolate.

"Malik – that was your Headteacher."

Malik stopped chewing. He turned pale, which Grandfather noticed.

"Very kind lady – wished to know how you were."

Malik blinked. "Did you say I was quite OK, Grandfather?"

Grandfather nodded. "But I myself will walk to school with you in future. Is good for my old legs."

Malik looked at him sideways.
Could Grandfather possibly have
guessed? "Thanks a lot, Grandfather."

Grandfather patted his hand. "And behave yourself, eh?"

So there were no more days for Jamie and Malik up the Patch, trying to tame Sultan. Instead they had to sit up front in class, and play baseball under a monitor's eye.

"I'll never tame that cat now," Jamie moaned to Jen.

"Try to lure him off the garden wall again," she suggested.

But Jamie knew Sultan didn't really like the garden. He preferred ferns and gorse bushes and the neighbours' she-cats. He liked to lie in the long grass, expose his fur belly to the sun, and catch butterflies with an idle paw.

"Maybe I could look for him on the Patch after school," he wondered.

"With Malik? Shall I come too?"

Jamie wasn't sure he wanted to go half shares in his only friend. However, what Jen wanted she usually got: look at Pepper. He sighed. "All right."

Visiting the Patch at that time of day was a failure, with the old men shuffling round looking for shelter, and noisy gangs from other schools fooling about. If the cat was there, he was in hiding.

"Let's go home," said Jamie despondently.

"Let's go to your house instead, Malik, and play chess," suggested Jen.

Jamie felt defeated. Just hope his mum doesn't kiss me, he thought. At least we might get something good to eat, though.

"Why, it is our Hero!" exclaimed the Chess Queen, folding him to her

bosom when they reached the shop.
"And this is little sister? My, my!" Jen
was embraced too. "How good you
bring her with you."

"Yes, that's Jen . . . she wants to
play chess with Malik."

"*Chess*? Women are too busy for
such nonsense. Go and find
Grandfather with Malik, Jamie, while
little Jen helps me with some tea."

Jen's mouth fell open as she was led
away. Jamie grinned. Malik looked at
him and shrugged.

"Come on out into the garden," he said.

"You've got a proper *garden*?" Jamie was envious.

"Yes – it's big – goes right down to the road." Malik proudly led the way to where Grandfather sat dozing beneath a cherry tree, with his turban slipped sideways. Mr Pradesh was lying back in a deck chair, looking up into the branches.

"Here's Jamie," said Malik. "He's brought his sister too."

Grandfather half-opened his eyes, and half-snored a greeting.

"My, it is our Hero," said Mr Pradesh. "You do not come yet to see my surgery, Jamie."

In all Jamie's troubles, the invitation had slipped his mind.

"Come Saturday, early. That is

when they bring me many, many patients."

"Fine. I'd like that."

Malik had already begun laying out the chessmen when his mother called to them, "Little Jen goes to bring your parents over, Jamie, so we may all meet."

A cloth was soon spread over a garden table, and by the time the Joneses arrived everything was ready for a feast of welcome. Then Malik's mother called her husband, and he closed the shop and brought out wine and fruit juice in case no one wanted tea.

"What a kind, relaxing treat," sighed Mum.

Malik ate delicately. Jen forgot the trampoline and Pepper, and stuffed herself like Jamie. Mr and Mrs Jones were ashamed of their twins' greed, but the Chess Queen was delighted. She hovered over them, pressing them to eat.

"Poor Pepper," Jamie teased Jen. He was licking his fingers – frowned upon by Mum – when he noticed something interesting at the bottom of the garden.

"Wow, that's some splendid kennel! Did Grandfather's dog live there?"

Malik nodded. "You never saw such a dog – feathery and silky, and ran like a racehorse, till he got older than Grandfather – for a dog, I mean." They thought about it, solemnly.

"Couldn't your grandfather have another dog?"

"He's too old now. All the trouble and exercise."

"Well . . . he could have an older

dog." What was that word Mum used? "*Mature.* We could walk it for him." Jamie thought about Barrel: everyone liked him, and he was perfectly mature. They might be surprised by him at first, but he was so appealing.

The more he thought about it, the more he knew it was the perfect solution all round. The difficult part might be getting other people to agree. People could be so thick about good schemes – as suspicious as Sultan. Dare he ask Grandfather straight out? He knew about Barrel already . . .

But Grandfather was dozing again, while Mr Pradesh talked happily to Mum. People always seemed to like her, almost as much as they liked Barrel. Perhaps she'd speak to Grandfather for him, later on?

He tried to catch her eye, without success. He sighed.

"Something the matter, Jamie?" asked Dad.

"Just thinking," he mumbled. He must be careful not to wind Dad up, or Mum might take his side. Dad mightn't like Barrel round the house again – even if he was living somewhere else.

What about asking Mr Pradesh on Saturday for help? He was an animal lover – and Grandfather's great friend . . .

"If you're not going to play chess with Malik, Jamie," said Jen impatiently, "I *am*."

Chapter Five

"YOU'RE UP VERY early today, Jamie," exclaimed Mum, handing him a bowl of cornflakes.

"Got some things to do."

"What sort of things?"

"Mr Pradesh said I could come and watch his early surgery."

The surgery was near the Patch, and Jamie thought he might find Sultan first. No need to tell Mum, though; she didn't like the Patch.

"Bacon, Jamie?"

"OK." He didn't want it – but the cat would.

It was good, out early. Air smelt better, clear and fresh. Up on the Patch the old men were still dozing, dew on their clothes. No one else was about. The hawk hovered, sharp-eyed for breakfast.

Jamie called, "Sul-tan! Ca-at!" And then "Ginger?" in case Sultan had forgotten his new name. But there was no flash of marmalade fur in the early sunshine. He sat down by the gorse bushes and waited. Nothing stirred.

Funny, there'd been no large stones lying about here before. He examined one closely, and found a dark red stain. That was odd, too. He stood up and peered beneath the bushes, parting the thorny branches.

The cat lay on his side, eyes closed. He was panting and his coat was dull, streaked with red. He was limp as an old rag.

"Oh . . . *Sultan.*"

A greengage eye half opened, stared, closed again. Jamie squatted down beside him. Very gently he ran one finger down Sultan's spine. The cat flinched but didn't try to pull away. A deep cut over his ribs gaped open.

"You're hurt! Who did it? I bet it was some filthy gang." Jamie eased his hands under the limp body. "Come on – must get you to Mr Pradesh somehow." But Sultan mewed feebly when Jamie tried to lift him, bit, struggled weakly, and crawled farther under the bush. One leg dragged sideways.

"*Stupid* cat – I'm trying to *help* you!" Jamie felt foxed but soon had an idea. He scoured the Patch till he found two long straight birch twigs. He pulled off his shirt and thrust them through its armholes to form a makeshift stretcher.

The next part would be harder, since Sultan had crawled so far under the bushes that Jamie got well pricked and torn before he was successful. Sultan spat, scrabbled and mewed as he was rolled on to the stretcher, but at last he was packaged into sausage-roll shape, the twigs held firmly together above his back. Only some angry whiskers could be seen, and the tip of a twitching tail. Treating him with great care, Jamie crawled out backwards.

It was already half-past nine when they reached the surgery, and there were quite a number of anxious owners waiting with their pets.

"We're busy today," said a fierce-looking receptionist in glasses.

"You'll have to wait. If it's minor, come back on Monday."

"It's very *un*minor. I'm Jamie Jones. Mr Pradesh said I could come and watch him in his surgery. And I've brought my cat; he's been very badly hurt. He's bleeding, and he's got a broken leg."

The woman leaned over to peer suspiciously into the sausage roll. In spite of his groggy condition Sultan gave her back the look of a cat that stands no nonsense.

"You see?" demanded Jamie. "He's bad. I told you."

"Um, perhaps . . . " She retreated and spoke into her intercom. "Sir, there's a boy here says you promised to let him watch you in the surgery . . . Yes, Jamie Jones. He's brought a cat that he says is badly hurt. Broken leg.

Bleeding."

Mutter, mutter the other end. Some muttering in the room behind Jamie too.

"Very well. You can go straight through," the receptionist told Jamie, pointing. "Mr Pradesh will see your cat the moment he's through with his present patient."

"*Brilliant*," gasped Jamie, gratefully.

"Hello, Jamie." Mr Pradesh greeted him without looking up. Dressed in a clean white coat, he was busy putting a bandage on a hamster's front leg. "I hear you bring me a patient. It is your wild cat, eh? I will be with him in just one moment. By the way, this is my assistant, Sally."

Sally had her hands cupped round the hamster. It was very good, and only made a small, sad noise when given an injection.

"Was your cat mauled? Run over?" asked Mr Pradesh.

"A gang stoned him, I think. He's badly cut, and one leg's sort of sideways."

Mr Pradesh put the hamster into a box with airholes, and handed it to the waiting owner, saying, "Bring him back Monday, for a check-up.

Now, Jamie, give me the cat."

All his movements were very quick and deft as he extracted Sultan from his wrappings and placed him gently on the table, stroking him from head to tail. Sultan didn't even try to bite – though his tail twitched as Mr Pradesh examined him with a featherlight touch, and he growled.

"He is very angry, which is a good sign. That he pants is natural; he has been shocked."

"Don't worry, Jamie," Sally whispered kindly. "He's a very good vet."

Jamie nodded, biting his fingernails.

"X-rays for the leg, I think, Sally," said Mr Pradesh.

"He *will* be all right, won't he?" asked Jamie tremulously.

"It is not too serious. The cut is

deep, yes – but we give him an injection, stitch and dress, and then set the leg. He must be nursed, of course. You were clever to get him here like this."

Jamie glowed. "*I* can nurse him."

"No, no. You are at school, and it needs skill. Mother is too busy. Sultan stays in hospital."

Jamie drooped. "Then I'll never tame him, will I?"

"A tom, and a confirmed stray, will never really tame now," said Mr Pradesh gently. But you can take him treats still."

It was a few minutes before Sally returned with the X-rays. In the meantime Mr Pradesh allowed Jamie to help him prepare the dressings. Soon Sultan was given the anaesthetic, his cuts stitched and dressed, and his leg set. Limper than ever, he was placed in a closed basket to sleep off the effects.

"There, I told you not to worry," said Sally, as the next patient was brought in: it was a collie, which growled as his owner lifted him on to the table.

Mr Pradesh only smiled, and stroked the collie's ears and throat. "You know how to tell a good vet,

Jamie?" he asked. "They have all their fingers!" He wriggled his own. Under his capable touch the collie lay down trustingly on the table.

Jamie was enthralled. Now that he had handed over responsibility for Sultan to Mr Pradesh, he was able to enjoy watching him at work. If he could only come and watch Mr Pradesh often it would be worthwhile living in town.

"I think I'll be a vet," he announced at last, after seeing Mr Pradesh treat a whole assortment of animals. "I'll be a country one, when I'm trained."

"An excellent decision. Now, would you hold this puppy while Sally gets his injection ready? He's our last patient today."

The puppy was warm and wriggling between Jamie's hands. "Wow! He's got sharp teeth – like pins! . . . Please, may I visit Sultan in hospital?" he begged, once the puppy had been taken away.

"Sally is my hospital. And a first-class one, too. Ask her." Mr Pradesh removed his white coat. "Now we reward ourselves with a cup of coffee, eh? Or better still, we will have it with my dear old friend, Malik's grandfather. Sally will lock up."

As they walked along together, Jamie thought it was just the right moment to broach his wily plan.

"Mr Pradesh, you know my dog Barrel that I was telling you about? He's special – he's beautiful, in an ugly way. I do miss him. And Malik's grandfather misses his dog still, doesn't he?"

Mr Pradesh nodded. "Yes, he is

very sad still, old Grandfather."

"Barrel would cheer him up no end, and he'd just fit into that empty kennel," said Jamie eagerly. "Their garden's so big, and Malik and I could walk him on the Patch. Would you ask Grandfather for me? *Please*?"

Mr Pradesh looked at him and smiled. He smiled often, like Malik. "I think you should ask him, Jamie. You are the Hero! And he has a heart of butter for Malik, his only grandchild."

Jamie looked sideways at him. He'd never felt quite easy about that day. Animals trusted Mr Pradesh, didn't they? They always knew. Perhaps he should tell Mr Pradesh everything about the wildcat strikes, and how Malik had got hurt.

When Jamie had finished, Mr Pradesh said, "Very wrong, all this

bunking off. Vets can't, you know. They have a duty." But his moustache twitched a bit. "And very very wrong, all this lying, eh?"

"Malik sort of stretched the truth a bit – I just let things happen. You won't give him away, will you?"

Mr Pradesh shook his head. "You tell Grandfather the truth, and then ask him about Barrel. You looked after Malik, anyway, didn't you?"

"Mm . . . I can't drop Malik in it, though."

"Grandfather is a very kind, understanding old man. I'm sure it will be all right, but you must decide, Jamie."

Jamie sighed. Exhausting, the way you had to do everything for yourself. Without Jen, either. He felt as old as Grandfather.

Jen and Malik were in the garden already, playing chess. Grandfather sat nearby, watching them with a smile.

"I've got Malik's Bishop," shouted Jen triumphantly.

Mr Pradesh approached Grandfather and said, "Now, our Hero wants to ask you something and tell you something. It is partly secret."

"If it is secret, we had better take a walk together, eh?"

Grandfather heaved himself out of

his chair. He took his knobbly stick in
one hand, and Jamie's arm in the
other.

They walked off down the garden
and stood looking at the flowers, while
Jamie talked about Barrel and the

difficulties of having such a small flat with no proper garden. "And he misses me, I'm sure he does." His voice trembled. "I know you must feel bad without Akbar – but Barrel would be so happy in your kennel. He's a comforting type of dog. You and Akbar wouldn't mind him there one bit. Even if Akbar was a ghost now, Barrel would be friendly to him. He's that sort."

Grandfather grunted. "Hm." He poked at the flower bed with his stick. He drew patterns on the earth. "You have asked for something, young man. Now, what were you to tell me?"

He listened, nodding gravely now and then, while Jamie retold his story. He said, "So?" and another time, "So!" Once he smiled, and muttered, "This – I almost guessed." When Jamie explained why Malik was afraid to tell the truth, he looked sad, shook his head, and murmured, "My son is a good man, a very good man – but sometimes hasty. I will choose my time to speak with him – and to tell Malik it is not good to lie. Come, Jamie, why do you tell me so much now?"

Jamie felt himself go scarlet. "Well, you see, you ought to know I'm not a hero, or anything like that. It would

have been a bit mean to get Barrel
back by – well, cheating."

"Yet you fought for Malik, anyway.
You brought him home safe to his

mother – who spoils him, as perhaps I do. 'One good turn – ' how does it go? Akbar was a wonderful dog, my great friend. I think he would forgive us both for putting Barrel in his kennel.''

Jamie choked. He flung his arms round Grandfather, hugging him so fiercely that they nearly toppled over into the flowerbed.

"Come, pick up my stick for me, and let us tell the others," said Grandfather.

They were all delighted, particularly Jen. Now perhaps Jamie would cheer up at last. "Shall I ask Pamela if she'll look round for another dog for Mr Bates?" she asked. "Then he won't mind losing Barrel."

"Anyone normal would mind losing Barrel," said Jamie. "But he's coming here if we have to kidnap him. I mean, dognap."

Grandfather smiled round at them indulgently. "It will be a great pleasure for me to make the acquaintance of so agreeable a dog," he said.

And Mr Pradesh added: "But don't let Barrel meet Sultan, Jamie. That might cause a different sort of wildcat strike, indeed!"